Shakespeare's
THEATRE

Andrew Langley

paintings by
June Everett

OXFORD
UNIVERSITY PRESS

For Pierre Andrieu, in gratitude.
J.E.

OXFORD
UNIVERSITY PRESS

Great Clarendon Street, Oxford OX2 6DP

Oxford University Press is a department of the University of Oxford.
It furthers the University's objectiive of excellence in research, scholarship,
and education by publishing worldwide in

Oxford New York

Athens Auckland Bangkok Bogotá Buenos Aires Calcutta
Cape Town Chennai Dar es Salaam Delhi Florence Hong Kong Istanbul
Karachi Kuala Lumpur Madrid Melbourne Mexico City Mumbai
Nairobi Paris São Paulo Singapore Taipei Tokyo Toronto Warsaw

with associated companies in Berlin Ibadan

Oxford is a registered trade mark of Oxford University Press
in the UK and in certain other countries

Published in the United States
by Oxford University Press Inc., New York

A CIP catalogue record for this book is available from the British Library

ISBN 0-19-910565-0 hardback
ISBN 0-19-910566-9 paperback

10 9 8 7 6 5 4 3 2

Typeset by Moondisks Ltd, Cambridge
Printed in Italy by G. Canale & C. S.p.A. - Borgaro T.se (Turin)

Contents

Introduction

One day in 1980, artist June Everett came upon a large open space on Bankside, opposite St Paul's Cathedral on London's River Thames. It was surrounded by derelict workshops; blackberry vines scrambled over rubble and rusty wheelbarrows. June decided to paint the scene, with its picturesque view of St Paul's in the distance, little knowing that this was to be the site of an astonishing feat of historical reconstruction. For this was the place chosen by American film director and actor Sam Wanamaker, for the rebuilding of Shakespeare's Globe Theatre.

June Everett met Wanamaker, who appointed her Artist of the Record for the project. Over the next 17 years she painted in meticulous detail every stage of the ambitious and complex operation. She recorded not only the faithful use of materials and techniques from Shakespeare's time, but also the people involved, from bricklayers and carpenters to plasterers, thatchers and, finally, actors. The result is an extraordinary collection of over 150 pictures, a selection of which appears in this book.

▲ *London in Shakespeare's time. The old cathedral of St Paul's stands on the north bank of the Thames. The original Globe can be seen at the bottom of the picture.*

▶ *The new Globe site at Bankside in 1980, seven years before the site was cleared. Wren's St Paul's is visible in the distance.*

In 1997, London's new Globe Theatre opened its doors with a performance of William Shakespeare's *The Two Gentlemen of Verona*. Situated on the south bank of the River Thames, the theatre stands near the site of the original Elizabethan Globe, where many of the greatest plays of Shakespeare were staged for the very first time. Shakespeare was one of the leading members of the company at the Globe – not just as playwright, but as actor and shareholder too.

There have been three Globe Theatres beside the Thames. The first was built in 1599, but it had a short life, burning to the ground in 1613. The theatre was immediately rebuilt, but this second Globe survived only slightly longer. In 1644 it was pulled down to make room for housing.

Then came three centuries of neglect. When the American actor Sam Wanamaker visited London in 1949, the only sign of the old Globe's existence was a blackened bronze plaque. He vowed that one day he would build a replica of the famous theatre. Thanks to Wanamaker's energy and inspiration, this third Globe has risen on Bankside, and its creation has taught us a vast amount about the theatre of Shakespeare's time.

Shakespeare first came to London in about 1587. After spending his early life at Stratford-upon-Avon, he had probably joined a company of players on their way to the capital. He saw a city which was growing rapidly. Overcrowded already, it had expanded beyond the medieval city walls to the north and east, and across the River Thames to the south.

The only way for wagons and walkers to cross to the south bank was over London Bridge. This had a gatehouse at one end, where the heads of executed traitors were put on display. In 1598 (the year before the first Globe was built), a German visitor counted over 30 heads on the bridge!

The ancient stone structure also had 19 small arches. These slowed the flow of the Thames so much that in very cold winters it froze over completely, and 'frost fairs' were held on the river itself. In 1683 a whole ox was roasted on the ice.

▶ *A wedding feast at Bermondsey on the south bank of the Thames in about 1570, in a painting by Joris Hoefnagel. The Tower of London can be glimpsed on the far left.*

▼ *Anchor Terrace on Bankside, seen through the window of a derelict house. The terrace today leads towards the Globe and contains the Anchor Inn, built in 1775.*

In early Elizabethan times, actors were thought of as little more than wandering troublemakers. A law passed in 1572 threatened punishment for any 'idle rogues and vagabonds', and forced players' companies to organize themselves properly. They had to obtain a licence to perform, and find a nobleman to be their patron, to provide financial support and protection.

The companies also had to earn enough money to make a living, buy costumes and props, and hire backstage hands. At this time there were few permanent theatres. Shakespeare probably began his career by joining a company of travelling actors. These companies performed their plays in village greens, inn-yards, schools, halls of great houses, and market places, like the one at Stratford, where Shakespeare would have seen plays as a boy. These spaces were usually open, and the audience did not pay to enter. Instead, the players passed round a hat after the performance.

This, however, was not a very reliable way of making money (spectators could easily slip away before the hat reached them). So enclosed playhouses were built, where customers had to pay to get in. The first of these were the Red Lion at Whitechapel in 1567, and the Theatre at Shoreditch in 1576. Neither has survived today, but they may have had galleries on three sides and a stage jutting out into the middle. By the end of the century, when Shakespeare was at the height of his career, playgoing had become a fashionable pastime.

23rd. April 1987.
George Inn. Southwark.
Romeo & Juliet.

▲ A performance of Romeo and Juliet *was given in 1987 at the George Inn, Southwark. This is the only remaining galleried inn in London. The aim was to raise funds desperately needed for the Globe project.*

 Bankside had been London's playground since the Middle Ages. It was part of the 'Liberty of the Clink', an area south of the Thames (opposite the present St Paul's Cathedral) and outside the direct control of the City's authorities. This meant that all sorts of entertainment could be found here which were frowned on, or even banned, north of the Thames. There were brothels and arenas for bull- and bear-baiting. There were no less than 22 inns. And there were four theatres, including the Globe itself.

The authorities especially disapproved of theatres – they enticed apprentices and artisans away from their work, and encouraged riotous behaviour. Some people believed plays were immoral: one author wrote 'a play is like a sink in a town, whereunto all the filth doth run'.

Bankside, however, belonged to the estate of the Bishops of Winchester, who did not object to playhouses or pubs. Not surprisingly, actors, managers and poets came to live here, enjoying the more free and easy atmosphere. By 1600 Shakespeare had probably moved across the river to the area to be nearer the Globe. Shakespeare's younger brother Edmund (an actor) is buried in nearby Southwark Cathedral, as are the dramatists John Fletcher and Philip Massinger.

◄ *Southwark Cathedral still has a close connection with the Globe. It contains a modern memorial and window dedicated to Shakespeare, and next to them a plaque in memory of Sam Wanamaker.*

How was the first Globe built? It was actually made from the parts of another playhouse called, simply, the Theatre. Founded in 1576, the Theatre had been the idea of James Burbage. Burbage began his working career as a carpenter, but he soon found the life of a 'common player' much more exciting. He saw, too, that money could be made from staging plays, and decided to build his own playhouse.

Burbage rented a plot of land in Shoreditch, outside London's city walls, and built a new playhouse of jointed oak timbers. We do not know what the Theatre looked like, but its shape was probably based on the round animal-baiting arenas which were popular at the time.

The Theatre flourished, and when Shakespeare came to London he joined Burbage's company. With successful plays and published poetry to his credit, he was clearly a writer of promise. Burbage died in 1597, and the lease for the Theatre ran out soon after. The owner of the land refused to renew it, and threatened to pull the building down.

Burbage's two sons Cuthbert and Richard acted quickly. Soon after Christmas 1598 they assembled a gang of helpers who pulled the Theatre apart, loaded the timbers onto boats and rowed them across the Thames. The owner was outraged, but too late. The Burbages had already leased another site on Bankside, and here they used the old timbers to erect a new playhouse – the Globe.

▶ *Work begins: the colourful ground-breaking ceremony for the new Globe in July 1987. It had taken this long for Wanamaker to raise the money and finalize his plans for the building. Here, the Duke of Edinburgh formally accepts the 24 main uprights of English oak, donated by 24 countries around the world. Oak was at the heart of the project, along with other traditional materials, including brick and thatch.*

When the original Globe was being erected, Bankside already boasted two playhouses. The first was the Rose, built in 1587 by a wealthy businessman, Philip Henslowe, and a grocer called John Cholmley. While Cholmley supplied the refreshments, Henslowe staged many great plays, among them two of Shakespeare's earliest, *Titus Andronicus* and *Henry VI*.

The other playhouse was the Swan, which opened in 1594. A Dutch visitor thought it 'of all the theatres, the largest and most distinguished'. But it had no regular company of actors, and after 1601 was used more often for fencing and prize-fights than for plays. When the first Globe burned down in 1613, Henslowe took advantage of the disaster by opening a fourth theatre in Bankside. This was the Hope,

▲ The foundations of the Rose Theatre were uncovered during demolition work in 1989. Immediately a campaign was launched to save the site, and although offices have now been built on it, the remains are carefully preserved.

◀ A contemporary drawing of the Swan Theatre. This was very similar to the Globe, with a projecting stage, open roof and galleries on three sides.

converted from a bear-baiting arena. Although Ben Jonson's *Bartholomew Fair* was first performed here, the Hope's theatrical life was short, and there are no records of plays after 1616.

A globe is round, of course. The name of the Globe Theatre was meant to announce that the whole round world could be represented by the actors inside. Shakespeare referred to the theatre as 'this wooden O', a kind of hollow circle. But the Globe was not exactly round, for the parts of its timber frame were straight. It was polygonal, or many-sided (today's Globe has 20 sides).

In Elizabethan times, the ground along Bankside was marshy and sometimes flooded by the Thames, so the Globe had to have solid foundations. Trenches were dug and filled with rubble stone. Wide brick walls were built on top of these, and then the base timbers of the huge framework rested on the walls. The yard inside (which was open to the elements) was covered with a mixture of ash, sand and hazelnut shells, through which rainwater quickly soaked away.

▲ *The Big Pour, July 1992. Workmen pour concrete onto the iron formwork, to create the base for the piazza on which the new Globe will stand.*

▲ *The original Globe, painted in the seventeenth century.*
The foundations of this building were found during
excavation work in the 1980s. This allowed the design team
to work out the exact dimensions of the old playhouse and
use them in the plans for the new Globe.

*'Can this cockpit hold
The vasty fields of France? or may we cram
Within this wooden O the very casques
That did affright the air at Agincourt?'*

 These are the opening words of Shakespeare's *Henry V* – one of the very first plays to be performed at the newly-finished Globe in 1599. The 'cockpit' and the 'wooden O' were of course the theatre itself. The players were the Chamberlain's Men, one of the two main actors' companies at that time in London. They had the protection of the Lord Chamberlain, an official of the court. Shakespeare was a member of the company and would have appeared with them in their frequent performances before Queen Elizabeth I.

The Chamberlain's Men now had their own theatre. The money for building it had been raised from leading members of the company. Cuthbert and Richard Burbage owned half of the shares, and the others were divided among five other 'sharers'. These included Shakespeare. He would grow richer from this investment than from his writings, eventually buying a large house and a large amount of land in Stratford.

◀ *Will Kempe was a famous comic actor, and one of the original sharers, with Shakespeare, in the Globe. He took the parts of some of Shakespeare's greatest clowns, including Dogberry in* Much Ado about Nothing.

▲ *The first Shakespeare play to be performed at the
new site, on the playwright's birthday, 23 April 1993.*
The Merry Wives of Windsor *was performed on the
half-completed stage in front of a specially invited
audience, to raise money for the project. It was a
huge success.*

The Chamberlain's Men had a priceless advantage over their rivals – the pen of William Shakespeare. The fame of his early work meant he would draw in audiences. Although we know little of his early life, once he was in London he seems to have quickly developed into the greatest poet and playwright of his age. While he was at the Globe, he wrote at least 12 of his finest plays, which contributed hugely to the playhouse's success between 1599 and 1613.

This was a new profession. Very few good English plays had existed, even in the 1570s. Since then drama had soared in popularity, and there was a massive demand for fresh work. But Shakespeare did not hurry his writing. He probably wrote in the relative peace of his lodgings in Bankside. His output of fewer than 40 plays is modest compared to someone like Thomas Heywood, who wrote or co-wrote well over 200.

Shakespeare's plays were not available for anyone else to read and perform. His scripts remained with the Chamberlain's Men, so that the public would have to come to the Globe to see them. Even so, some of his most popular plays, including *Henry V* and *Hamlet*, were pirated (crudely copied) and staged by rival companies.

▶ *A portrait, said to be of Shakespeare, by an unknown artist. No pictures of him were painted during his lifetime.*

▶ *The contents page of the first collected edition of Shakespeare's plays, published in 1623.*

The Burbage brothers hired a carpenter called Peter Street to rebuild the old oak frame of the Theatre on the Globe site. But this was not such a simple matter. The timbers had become very hard, and the joints and pegs which held them together might have been damaged in the rush to dismantle the frame. His biggest difficulty was fitting the timbers together again. As each one was a slightly different shape, it would have had its own special place in the framework. So it is likely that the Globe timbers were put together in just the same pattern as at the Theatre.

▶ ▼ *Assembling a roof beam for the modern Globe and marking out a timber before cutting joints. The dimensions of the framework were calculated to match the original.*

Green (new) timber was used to construct the new Globe. The carpenter, Peter McCurdy, selected standing oak trees, and had them felled, trimmed and sawn into the rough shapes needed. He and his men neatened up the timbers with axes and cut joints for slotting them together. Just as in Elizabethan times, the framework was first erected in the workshop, each timber marked, and then the whole lot taken to pieces. When it reached the site, it was easily reassembled in the same order.

◀ *The framework comes together, aided by a crane.*

▼ *Cutting joints in the timbers, which could then be slotted together and held in place with wooden pegs.*

Why did Elizabethan Londoners love the theatre so much? After about 1600, as many as 15,000 people went to the city's playhouses every week. The main reason was that plays were exciting. For one penny, you could leave behind the drab, overcrowded, plague-ridden streets of London and enter a world of marvels and romance. Many of Shakespeare's plays were set in exotic places such as Venice, Bohemia or Ancient Egypt. There were swordfights, clowns and pitched battles, love scenes and songs, ghosts and witches.

Above all, there was colour. The Globe used no painted scenery on movable 'flats', but its stage was gorgeously decorated. Massive painted pillars held up the stage canopy, where the ceiling was bright with sun, moon and signs of the zodiac. At the back of the stage were the hangings, often depicting scenes from allegory.

◄ *'Rose-cheeked Adonis hied him to the chase': a scene from Shakespeare's poem* Venus and Adonis, *portrayed on one of the four richly embroidered new stage hangings presented by New Zealand.*

▼ *The Duke of Edinburgh accepts the New Zealand hangings on behalf of the Globe in April 1994. By now the concrete foundations of the site and most of the brick supporting walls have been completed.*

▲ *Traditional building techniques and materials have been used in the new Globe, but the new thatch is well protected against fire. Above it poke the heads of the automatic sprinkler system. The central yard is, of course, unroofed as in the original Globe.*

The builders of the original Globe wanted a theatre that was cheap and quick to erect. The massive oak frame was covered with lath and plaster. Workmen nailed thin laths of split timber to the frame, then filled the gaps between them with a plaster of sand and lime mixed with goat- or horse-hair.

Meanwhile thatchers worked on the gallery roofs (a Swiss visitor in 1599 called the Globe 'the house with the thatched roof'). They laid bundles of straw or locally-cut reeds, one above the other, and fixed them with wooden pegs or tarred twine. The thatch kept out the rain and kept in the warmth, but it had one huge disadvantage: it caught fire easily. This was to cause the Globe's disastrous end.

▼ *Plastering between the laths. On the right, a worker sprays the bare laths with water so that the plaster will not crack.*

▲ *A thatcher at work. The Norfolk reeds are treated with fire-proofing chemicals; beneath them is a flame-retardant board that is backed with foil.*

The cheapest way to see a play at the Globe was to be a groundling. For one penny, you could enter through the door leading into the yard around the stage. Here you would stand, jostled by up to 800 fellows. Groundlings included all sorts of people, from apprentices and soldiers to pickpockets and prostitutes.

For two pennies, you could pass through another door and up a set of stairs to the galleries. This payment only got you a hard and backless wooden seat, but at least you were safe from the rain. Your companions might be middle-class merchants or law students.

For three pennies or more, you could sit on a cushion in a more private part of the galleries near the stage. These were the most expensive seats, which only courtiers or members of noble families could afford.

▲ *The new balusters were all carved by one woman on a traditional pole lathe, powered by a treadle and a springy sapling.*

◀ *Oak balusters on the middle gallery of the new Globe. They were copied from a single original found during excavations at the Rose Theatre.*

▲ *A view from Bankside of the new Globe nearly completed, in July 1995.*
Work continues on the stage. The exterior of the theatre, with its limewashed walls,
is a conspicuous landmark – despite the office blocks surrounding it.

Bankside, with its theatres, inns and brothels, drew customers like a magnet. Most of them came over the river from the City of London on the north bank. The wealthiest were rowed in their own boats, and the less grand hired a wherry, or water taxi, to carry them over. Even those who walked across London Bridge had to pay a toll.

Thomas Platter, on a visit from Switzerland, went to the Globe in September 1599. He wrote, 'After lunch, about two o'clock, I and my party crossed the water, and there in the house with the thatched roof witnessed an excellent performance of the tragedy of *Julius Caesar*... Thus daily at two in the afternoon, London has two, sometimes three plays running in different places, competing with each other...'

The Globe's season probably began in September, and went on through the winter. This was often the only period when theatres were allowed to open. The heat of summer encouraged the spread of the plague in London's cramped streets, and public buildings were often closed. The Chamberlain's Men would spend the summer touring the country

▶ An Elizabethan ferryman rows some wealthy passengers across the Thames. Old London Bridge, with its gatehouse, can be seen in the background.

Going on stage at the Globe was a daunting experience. The actor entered upstage, from one of the three doors at the back. There was the stage, jutting out into the middle of the yard. It was about the size of half a tennis court and bare except for a few props. And there was the audience - not just in front of him, but on his right and left as well. He was almost surrounded, with 3,000 eager pairs of staring eyes. With no stage lighting, he could see the audience as clearly as it could see him.

There was no respectful hush. People carried on talking, eating, drinking, thieving and sometimes fighting. (Once, when the crowd caught a pickpocket, they tied him to one of the stage pillars as punishment.) They cheered or hissed the actors when they felt like it, and one poet wrote that there were 'shouts and claps at ev'ry little pause'. Some of the groundlings leaned on the front of the stage. If an actor moved too near them, they sometimes grabbed at his ankles!

Even more off-putting were the 'gallants', in the most expensive seats in the gallery rooms. Being so near the stage, they could distract the audience by making fun of the actors.

◄ *Groundlings watch a performance of* Henry V *on the stage of the modern Globe. As in Elizabethan times, there is a lot of interchange between the audience and the actors.*

◄ *Founder's Day: a bust of the late Sam Wanamaker is unveiled on his birthday, 14 June 1996. After many years of single-minded endeavour, he had not lived to see the final fulfilment of his dream. He died in 1993.*

As one of the Chamberlain's Men, Shakespeare had to work very hard. In one season, he and his colleagues would put on an average of 17 new plays, plus some old favourites. In a single week, they might present as many as six different plays. But it was a small company, with eight sharers and a few hired actors: Thomas Platter reckoned on 15 altogether when he came to the Globe in 1599. This meant that no-one could take a rest – not even the leading actors. Richard Burbage usually took all the lead roles for the Chamberlain's Men, including those of Hamlet, Othello and King Lear.

When did they find time to rehearse? In the afternoons the actors were on stage, while the evenings were too dark for working. That left the mornings for rehearsing a new play, as well as fitting costumes, preparing for the daily performance and making scenery. With such a packed programme, the actors probably had to

◀ *Characters from* The Two Gentlemen of Verona, *presented at the Globe in August 1996.*

▲ *Travelling players perform at a nobleman's house.*

learn their lines in private and only practised together on two or three occasions. Somehow, Shakespeare did all this and more. He did not take lead roles, but he usually played important parts, including that of the Ghost of Hamlet's father. He wrote a string of hugely successful plays. And he must have made regular visits to his family back in Stratford. In about 1610, he is thought to have retired there almost permanently, and he wrote nothing new after 1612.

 Behind the stage was the tiring house, or dressing room. Here the players put on costumes and make-up, stored their props and waited to go on stage. Here also stood the book-keeper, who prepared the acting copies of each play, and prompted actors when they forgot their lines. The tireman helped to dress the actors and move props. So the tiring house was a bustling place, crammed with clothing, hats, musical instruments, swords, copies of lines pasted onto parchment and, of course, nervous actors.

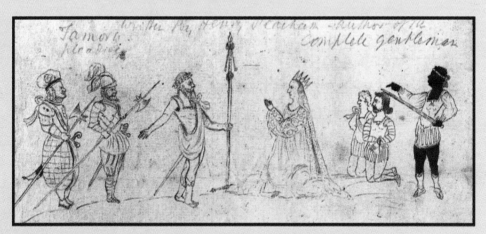

Acting companies kept a huge number of props and pieces of stage furniture. Here are some of the more surprising items kept by the company of the Admiral's Men in 1599: one bedstead, two steeples, one lion skin, one Hell mouth, Neptune's fork, two moss banks and one snake, Mercury's wings, one chain of dragons, one ghost's crown, one black dog.

▲ *A drawing of a scene from* Titus Andronicus, *made in about 1595.*

◄ *The frame for the tiring house at the new Globe. It is modelled as closely as possible on the original, and used in much the same way.*

39

In Shakespeare's *Hamlet*, when the Ghost urges the Prince to swear vengeance, its voice comes from beneath the stage. 'You hear this fellow in the cellarage!' cries Hamlet. To Elizabethan playgoers, the area under the stage represented Hell, a place for ghosts and demons. The stage itself was the Earth, where humans lived. Above it were the 'Heavens',

a huge canopy painted to represent the sky, sun and moon, with symbols for the heavenly bodies. Gods and goddesses could be flown, or lowered, through a trapdoor.

▲ *The new 'Heavens', with a trapdoor in the centre.* (Inset left) *Decorating the carved tops of the pillars with gold leaf, just as an Elizabethan craftsman would have done.* (Inset right) *Painting the frieze above the stage.*

'A dull Audience of Stinkards sitting in the penny-galleries of a Theatre and yawning upon the Players.' This is how one of Shakespeare's contemporaries described the customers at a playhouse. Another saw the audience as a wild beast which the actors had to tame. In an open theatre like the Globe, this was often a hard job.

Playgoers had to use their imaginations, spurred on by the power of Shakespeare's words, which conjured up a much bigger world. In *Henry V*, the Chorus tells them:

> 'Suppose within the girdle of these walls
> Are now confined two mighty monarchies,
> Whose high-upreared and abutting fronts
> The perilous narrow ocean parts asunder'.

In this way, a mostly bare stage could become a royal palace, a battlefield, a London tavern and many other places within a single play.

There also had to be action – lots of it. Shakespeare filled his plays with a huge amount of varied movement. The actors were constantly mobile, using the whole stage to draw in the spectators on each of the three sides. The two double entrance doors were used in many different ways. They could represent the English and French camps in *Henry V*. Actors coming in at one door and exiting by the other could suggest a march. Actors could hide in the curtained space at the back (as Hamlet does), or appear on the gallery above.

▲ *The stage is strewn with rushes for the beginning of the first performance of* Henry V.

▶ *The frenzied rush to finish work on the new stage, just a week before opening in May 1997.*

▲ *Spectators arrive at the new Globe on a fine afternoon in June 1997. This remarkable theatre is now a thriving and extraordinary part of Britain's artistic life. It is still expanding – an indoor theatre is being built for winter performances.*

For a decade, the Globe was London's leading theatre. Crowds flocked to enjoy a remarkable sequence of new plays and revivals staged by the King's Men (the new title of the Chamberlain's Men, after James I became King). During 1606, for example, they presented four great masterpieces – *King Lear* and *Macbeth* by Shakespeare, *Volpone* by Ben Jonson, and *The Revenger's Tragedy* by Cyril Tourneur.

But things were about to change. In 1608 the King's Men began to give performances at the private, indoor Blackfriars Theatre. At about this time, Shakespeare retired from the stage and eventually returned to live in Stratford-upon-Avon.

Then came the disaster of 1613. During a performance of *Henry VIII*, a piece of smouldering wadding from the stage cannon drifted onto the roof. All eyes of the 3,000 spectators were on the play, so none spotted any danger until the thatch burst into flames and the fire raced over the whole building. Amazingly, the audience escaped unscathed, except for a boy who had his breeches set on fire (which he doused with a bottle of ale). The Globe was burned to the ground in less than an hour.

Important dates in Shakespeare's life

(Most of the definite facts about Shakespeare come from official documents, not first-hand accounts)

1564 Baptised in Stratford-upon-Avon

1582 Married, in Stratford, to Anne Hathaway

1583 Daughter Susanna baptised

1585 Twins Hamnet and Judith baptised

1585-1586 Shakespeare goes to London and probably joins an actors' company

1589-1591 First plays written and performed, probably *Henry VI Parts 1, 2 and 3*, and *Titus Andronicus*

1592 Shakespeare's reputation grows: he is attacked by another writer, Robert Greene

1593-1594 The poems *Venus and Adonis* and *The Rape of Lucrece* are published

1595 Named as one of the Lord Chamberlain's Men appearing in plays before Queen Elizabeth

1596 Son Hamnet dies; rents lodgings in Bankside

1597 Buys New Place and an acre of land in Stratford

1598 His name appears as author of *Richard II, Richard III* and *Love's Labour's Lost*

1599 Globe Theatre opens: Shakespeare becomes a sharer

1601 Shakespeare's father dies: first performance of *Hamlet*

1602 Buys more land in Stratford

1603 James I succeeds Elizabeth I; Burbage, Shakespeare and company become the King's Men

1604 The King's Men take part in James I's coronation procession

1607 Brother Edmund dies and is buried at Southwark

1608 Shakespeare's mother dies: the King's Men begin performances at the (indoor) Blackfriars Theatre, in which Shakespeare has a one seventh share

1609 Volume of Sonnets published

1610 Shakespeare probably settles back in Stratford

1613 The first Globe burns down; last plays completed

1616 Signs his will; dies 23 April

Shakespeare's plays

(In approximate order of first performance)

Henry VI Parts 1, 2 and 3
Titus Andronicus
Richard III
The Comedy of Errors
The Taming of the Shrew
The Two Gentlemen of Verona
Love's Labour's Lost
Romeo and Juliet
Richard II
A Midsummer Night's Dream
King John
The Merchant of Venice
Henry IV Parts 1 and 2

Much Ado About Nothing
The Merry Wives of Windsor
Henry V
As You Like It
Julius Caesar
Twelfth Night
Hamlet
Troilus and Cressida
All's Well That Ends Well
Othello
Measure For Measure
Timon of Athens
King Lear

Macbeth
Coriolanus
Antony and Cleopatra
Pericles
Cymbeline
The Winter's Tale
The Tempest
Henry VIII
The Two Noble Kinsmen
(disputed authorship)

The main London theatres of Shakespeare's time

Opened in

1567	The Red Lion, Whitechapel
1576	The Theatre, Shoreditch
	The Blackfriars, Blackfriars
1577	The Curtain, Shoreditch
1587	The Rose, Bankside
1595	The Swan, Bankside
1599	The Globe, Bankside
1600	The Fortune, Clerkenwell
1602	The Boar's Head, Whitechapel
1604	The Red Bull, Clerkenwell
1614	The Hope, Bankside
1616	The Cockpit, Westminster

The new Globe Theatre

Shakespeare's Globe, New Globe Walk, Bankside, London SE1 9DT

The performance season at Shakespeare's Globe runs from May to September. The programme of plays for the forthcoming season is available from February, and advance booking opens then.

The Globe Exhibition is open all year round. It tells the remarkable story of the reconstruction of the theatre, and includes a guided tour.

The Shakespeare's Globe education programme includes lectures, tours, seminars and workshops, including ChildsPlay, special workshops for children based on the plays in performance. Full details can be obtained from the Globe Education Centre, Bear Gardens, London SE1 9ED.

Index

Page numbers in *italics* refer to pictures or their captions.

Acknowledgements

The publisher would like to thank the following for permission to reproduce photographs:

6–7 British Library; 8–9 Marquess of Salisbury; 16 Fotomas Index; 19 British Museum; 20 Mary Evans Picture Library; 23t National Portrait Gallery; 23b Fotomas Index; 26 Brett Robertson; 28 Tiffany Foster; 30–31 Wendy Cafferty; 33 Edinburgh University Library; 34–5 John Tramper; 37 British Library; 39 Marquess of Bath; 40–41, 42–43 Richard Kalina.